Mr. Magorium's Wonder Emporium

Scholastic Inc.

New York Toronto London Auckland Sydney
Mexico City New Delhi Hong Kong Buenos Aires

WALDEN.COM/MAGORIUM and MAGORIUM.COM

ISBN 13: 978-0-439-91251-8
ISBN 10: 0-439-91251-2

This book is published in cooperation with Walden Media, LLC.
Walden Media and the Walden Media skipping stone logo are trademarks and registered trademarks of Walden Media, LLC, 294 Washington Street, Boston, Massachusetts 02108.

Published by Scholastic Inc. All rights reserved.
SCHOLASTIC and associated logos are trademarks and/or registered trademarks of Scholastic Inc.

Book design by Rick DeMonico
Illustrations by Michael Massen
Photography by Kim Brown

12 11 10 9 8 7 6 5 4 3 2 1 7 8 9 10/0

Printed in the U.S.A.
First printing, October 2007

Dear Reader:

You are holding in your hands a volume prepared by Mr. Edward Magorium, the proprietor of Mr. Magorium's Wonder Emporium. Mr. Magorium had been making and selling (and talking to and occasionally having lunch with) toys for over two hundred years.

His first known toy invention was something he called a "creased contraption of gossamer aviation," now known as a paper airplane. In 1824, Magorium sold these paper airplanes at a booth in a traveling carnival, the sort then popular in Europe. His incredible contraptions caught the eye of the Royal Prince, and soon Magorium was appointed toymaker to the king. He continued to perfect his paper airplanes over the years and recorded his designs in notebooks that are currently stored in the Wonder Emporium's library.

In keeping with Mr. Magorium's love of play and fun, Ms. Mahoney has instructed me to make these designs available to young people. What follows are the original plans written by Mr. Magorium. I have taken the liberty of adding my own notes to each page.

Very truly yours,

Bellini

Bellini

THE MIRACLE OF FLIGHT

CREASED CONTRAPTIONS OF GOSSAMER AVIATION

By Edward Magorium

In the years since I created and sold my very first toy, a creased contraption of gossamer aviation, I have worked to perfect the process. Of course, I cannot take all the credit. It has often been the contraptions themselves who have told me when I was in error and encouraged me when I was doing something right. As you begin exploring the wonders of flight, I suggest that you always listen to your contraptions as you can learn a lot from a carefully folded piece of paper, or any piece of paper, for that matter.

Use printer paper, construction paper, or the paper in the back of the book to make your planes, and please consider the following instructions. They will help you to make contraptions that fly high and long.

- Fold your contraptions very carefully. All edges must line up exactly.
- You might want to practice making your contraptions on a piece of plain paper first, and then recreate it on the printed paper provided.
- Make your creases very sharp! Once you have lined up the edges, use the edge of a ruler to make the crease.
- As you fold, you may see some bulges along the creases, especially if there are several folds of paper. Take the time to smooth these out.
- Check the angle of your contraption's wings. They should rise above the body of the plane, not droop down.
- Your contraption must be symmetrical, that is, one side must be exactly the same as the opposite side. This is especially important when making wing folds.
- If your contraption has narrow wings, throw it faster. If it has large, wide wings, throw it slower.

DESIGN #1

The ARROW

THIS PLANE FLIES LIKE AN ARROW; FRUIT FLIES LIKE A BANANA. WHO DOESN'T LIKE A NICE BANANA EVERY NOW AND THEN?

1

Take one sheet of paper and fold it in half the long way to make a crease, then unfold it.

2

Fold the short edge of one side down to the center, lengthwise fold. Do this for the other side, too.

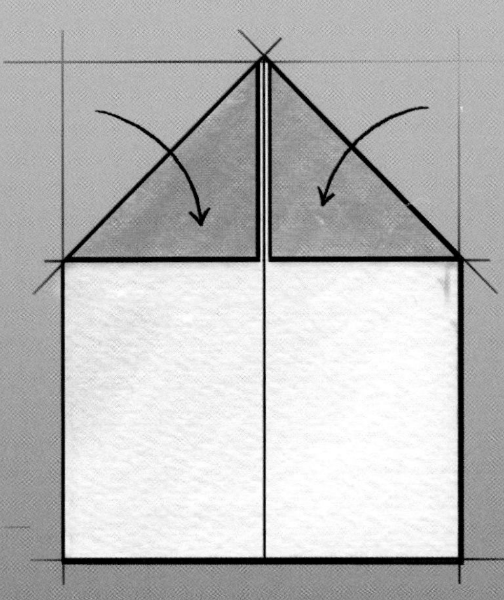

Early airplane engineers used paper airplanes as a way to experiment with wing and body shape and how they affected the ability to stay aloft.

Paper airplanes are listed in Mr. Magorium's Wonder Emporium's big book under three letters: under A for airplanes, P for planes, and C for creased contraptions of gossamer aviation.

3

Fold down the new fold you have created to the original fold you did in the first step. Do this for the other side, too.

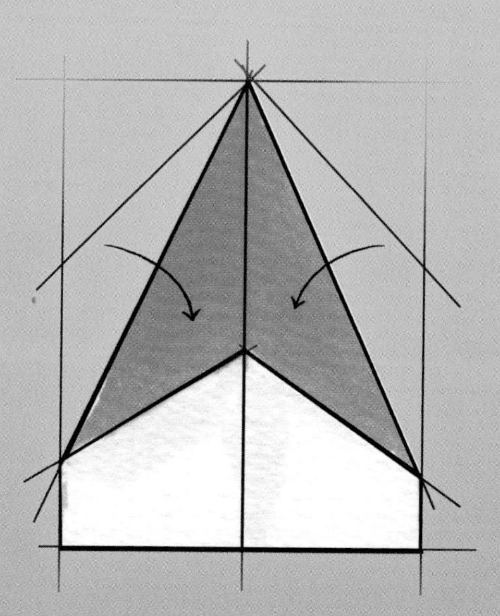

4

Hold by the underside of the plane. Open the wings out and away from the underside.

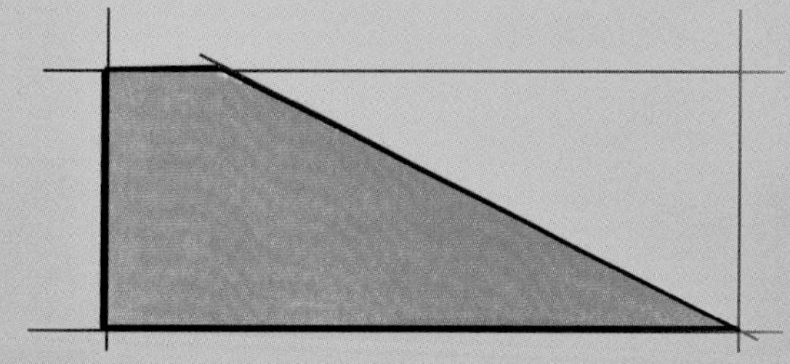

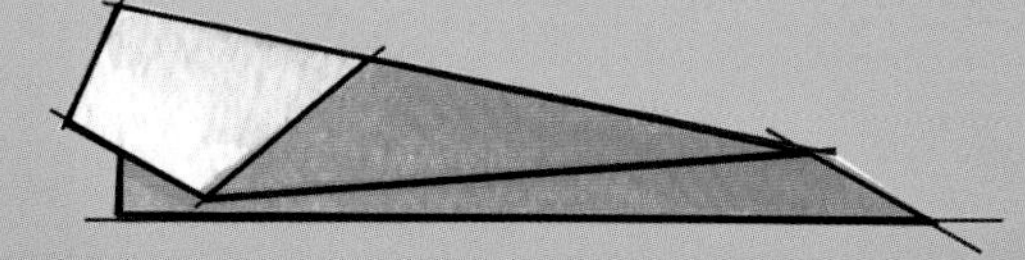

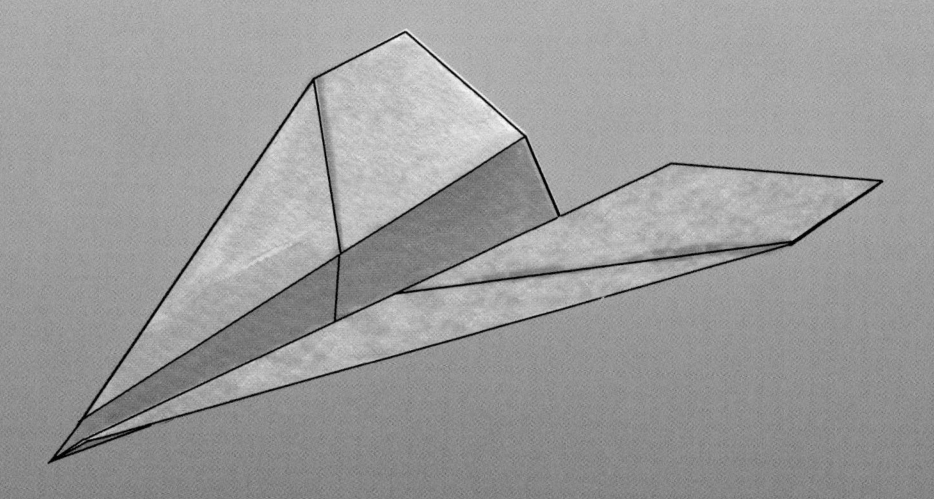

DESIGN #2

The CROWN

THIS CONTRAPTION ISN'T A TRADITIONAL PAPER AIRPLANE BUT FLIES WELL, ONCE YOU GET THE HANG OF HOW TO THROW IT.

1

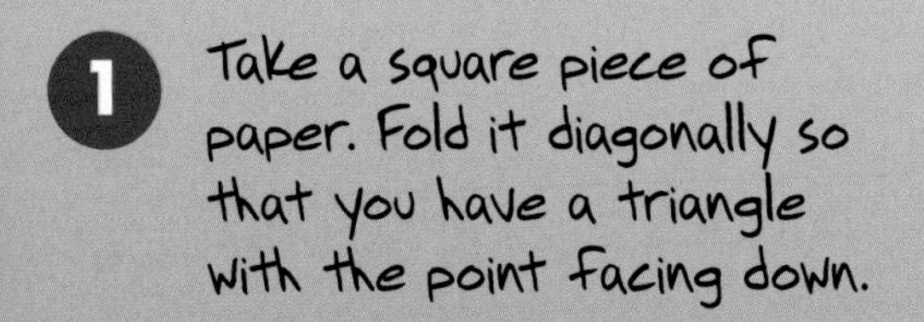

Take a square piece of paper. Fold it diagonally so that you have a triangle with the point facing down.

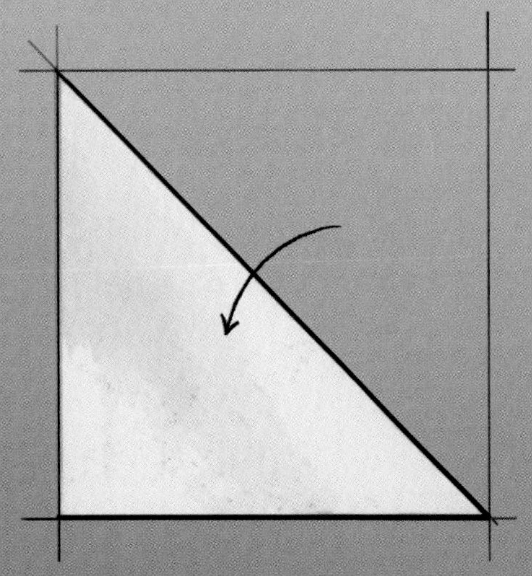

2

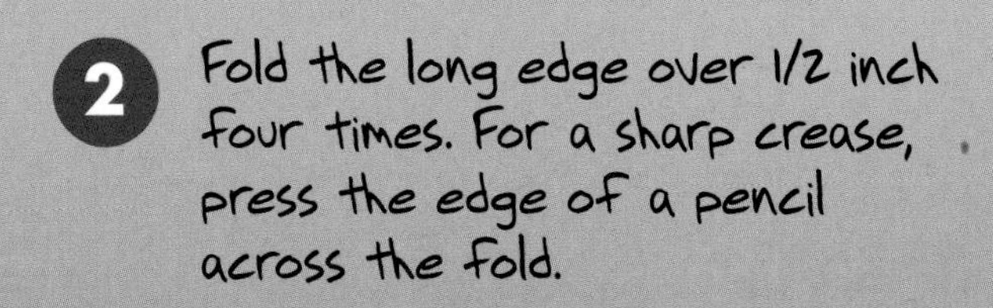

Fold the long edge over 1/2 inch four times. For a sharp crease, press the edge of a pencil across the fold.

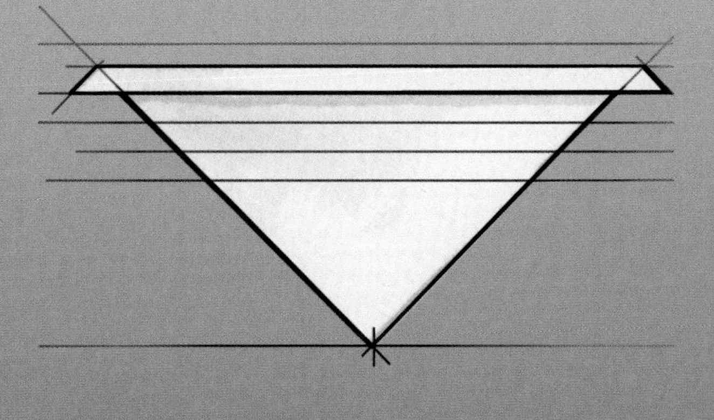

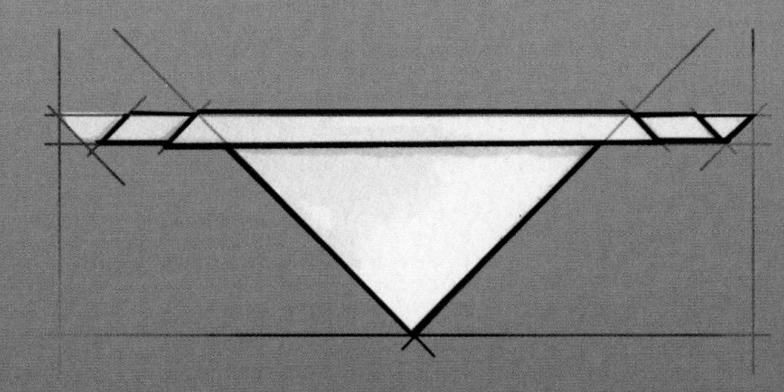

The kite is an ancestor of the paper airplane. The first kites were made 2,000 years ago in China.

3 Gently curl the long edges together so that they form a circle. Make sure the folded edge is on the inside of the circle.

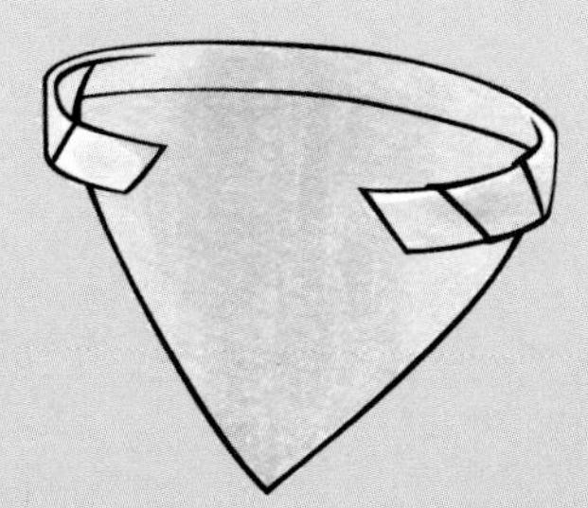

4 Slide the ends of the folded edges into each other to form a ring. Go over the long folded edge again to make it a perfect circle.

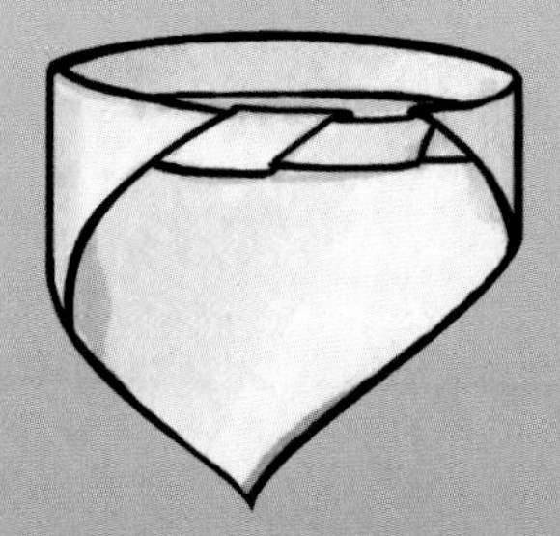

The mezzanine where the children's books are kept at Mr. Magorium's Wonder Emporium is an excellent place to launch a paper airplane.

5 Roll the tip of the pointed edge up around a pencil so that the curved piece points away from the ring. Unroll it and cut a slit from the pointed edge up towards the fold about one inch long.

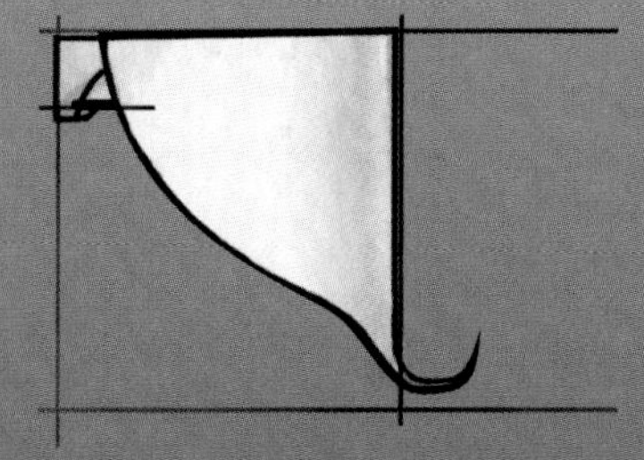

DESIGN #3

The ACCORDION

THIS CONTRAPTION REMINDS ME OF AN ACCORDION, ALTHOUGH I'VE ONLY MET ONE ACCORDION THAT COULD FLY MORE THAN A FEW FEET WITHOUT STOPPING TO CATCH ITS BREATH.

1

Take one sheet of paper and fold it in half the long way to make a crease, then unfold it.

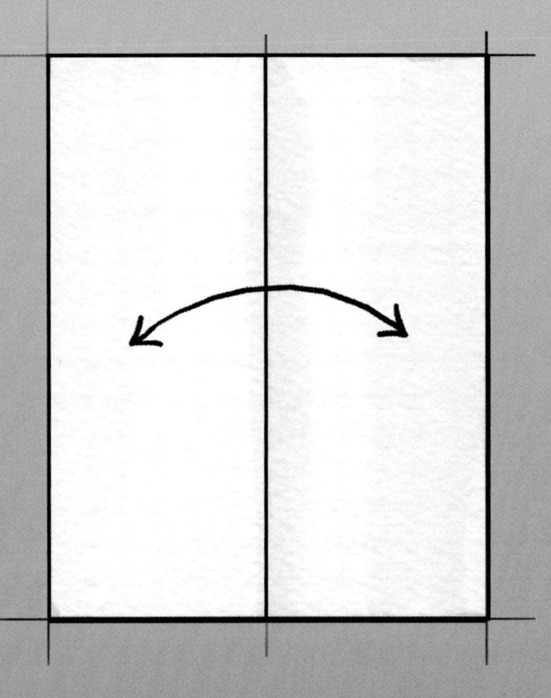

2

Fold the two top edges of the paper into the center fold, creating a point.

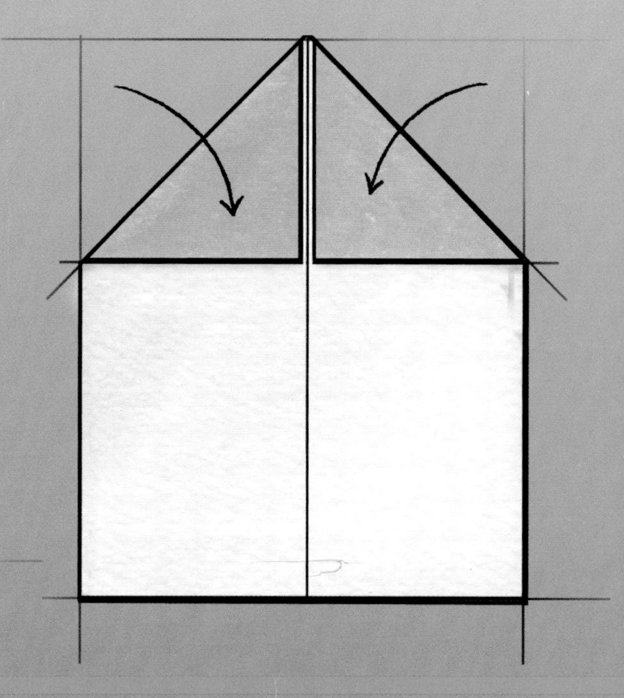

3

Fold the point down so that the top of the paper is flat.

4

Flip over, and fold the two top edges into the center fold creating a point. (Every time you do this the paper gets shorter.) Flip back.

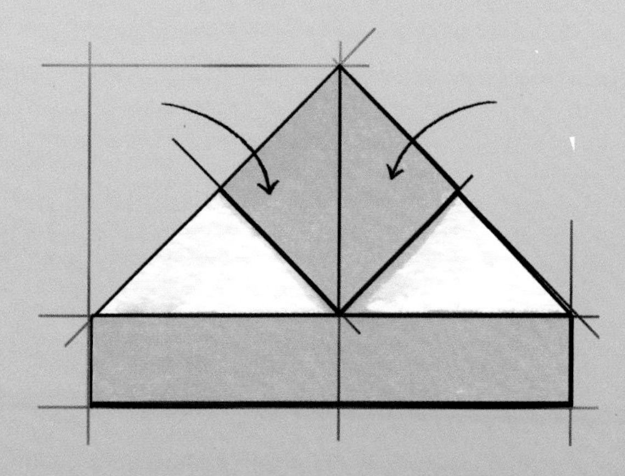

5

Fold the point down so that it matches the point that is already on that side. The edges should line up.

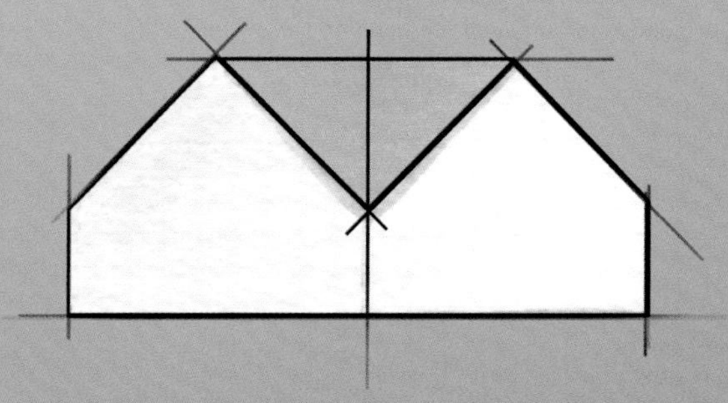

Paper airplanes will fly better if you add weight to the front. Try taping a paper clip to the nose inside the fold.

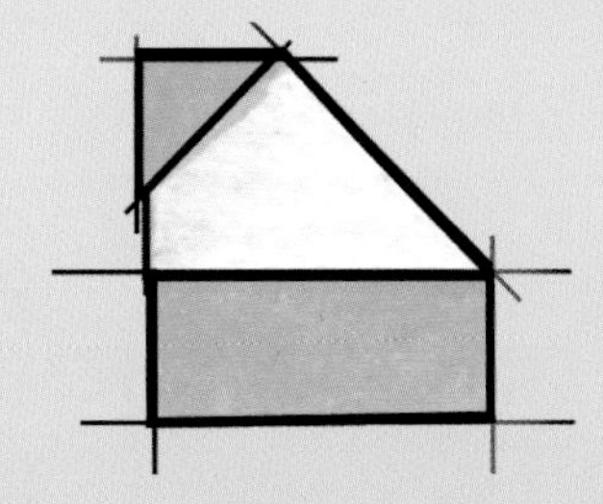

Close the plane along the center fold.

Fold down about an inch from the center fold. This forms the largest part of the wing. Make another fold an inch from the edge of the wing, angled up. This forms the outer edge of the wing. Repeat on the other side.

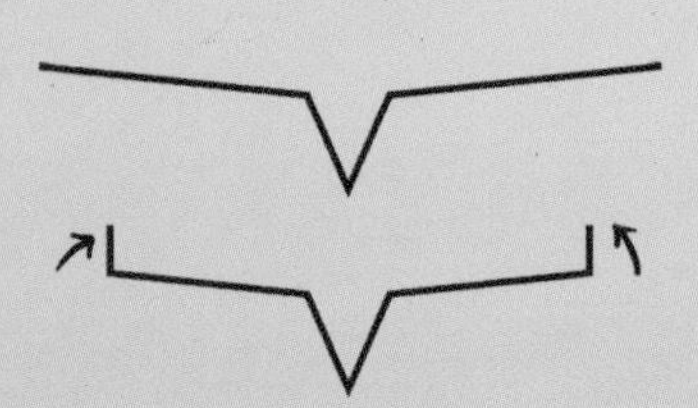

Mr. Magorium's planes were known to fly all by THEMSELVES if they felt like it. I often wondered if this was because Mr. Magorium talked to them. There's no way to even know if it will help your planes fly, but try having a little conversation with them. Even a "hello, how are you?" might make them fly a bit farther.

DESIGN #4

THE GRAVITY KILLER

THIS PLANE FLIES AS IF GRAVITY DIDN'T EXIST.

1. Take one sheet of paper and fold it in half the long way to make a crease, then unfold it.

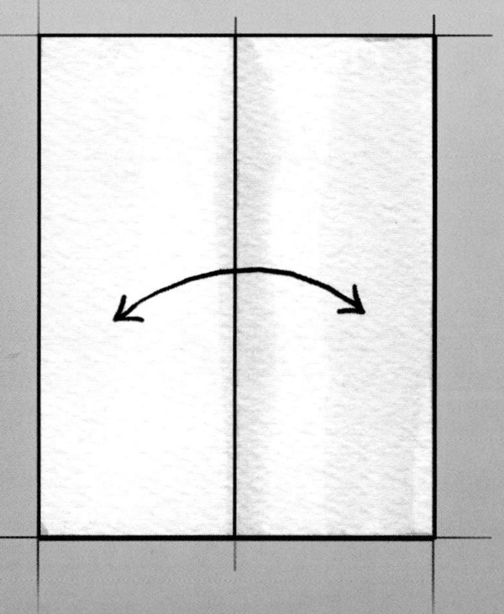

As of November 2006, Ken Blackburn holds the world record for longest flight by paper airplane: 27.6 seconds.

2 Make a fold of about one inch from the bottom of the paper. Make sure to place the center crease exactly on top of itself.

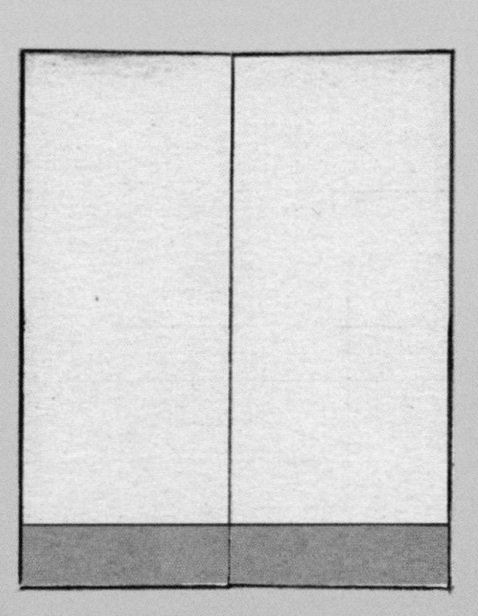

3 Do this same fold six times, being sure to line up the center creases each time. When you are done your paper should be approximately two inches tall.

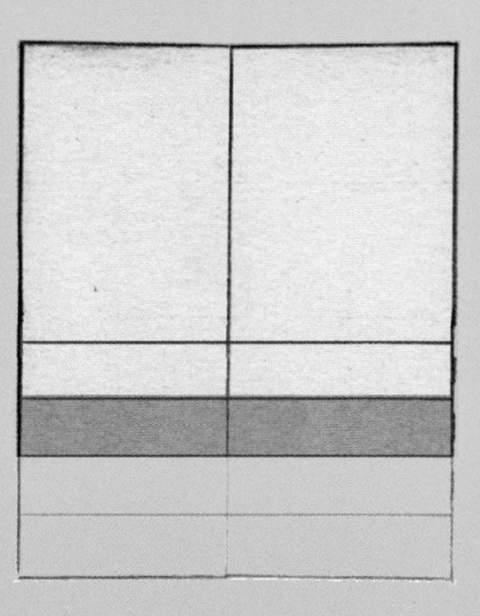

4 Flip the paper over and fold in half from left to right.

The art of making paper airplanes is sometimes called *aerogami*, after the Japanese word *origami*, for creating sculpture with folded paper.

Airplanes fly better if you believe in them. (And follow the directions carefully.)

5 Make a crease running top to bottom about one inch from fold.

6 Flip over and do the same thing on the other side.

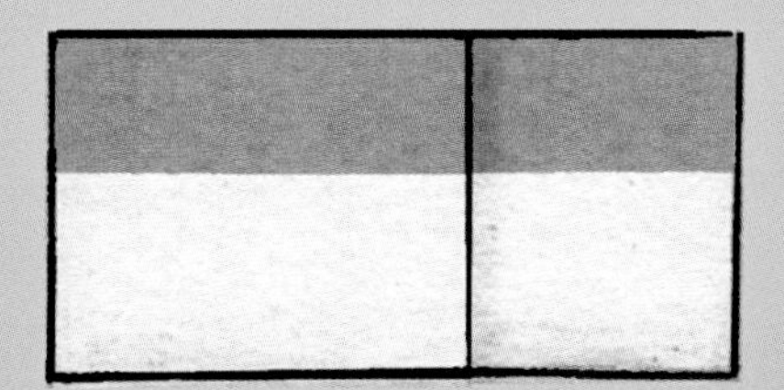

7 Make a fold about one inch from outer edge of wing so that the edge points up. Do the same thing on the other side.

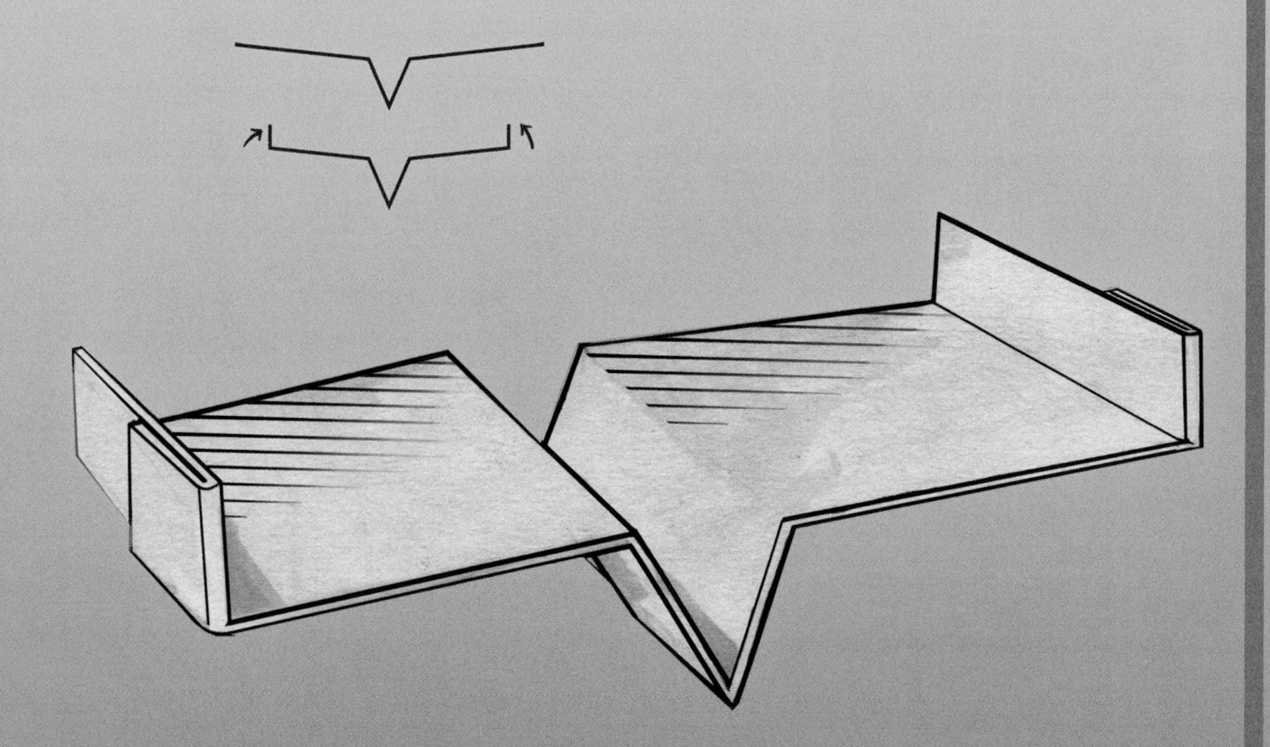

The ANGEL

THIS CONTRAPTION LOOKS AND FLIES LIKE AN ANGEL.

1

Take one sheet of paper and fold it in half the long way to make a crease, then unfold it.

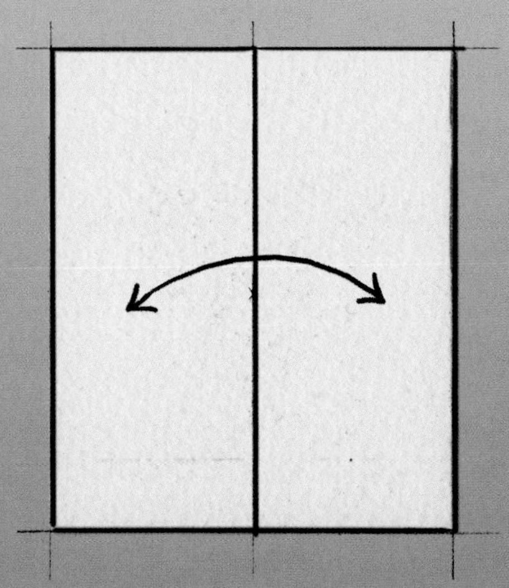

2

Fold the upper right corner down so the top edge is right on your center crease. Do the same thing to the other side.

3

Fold the top point down so that you are folding the paper left to right along the bottom edge of the flaps you just folded.

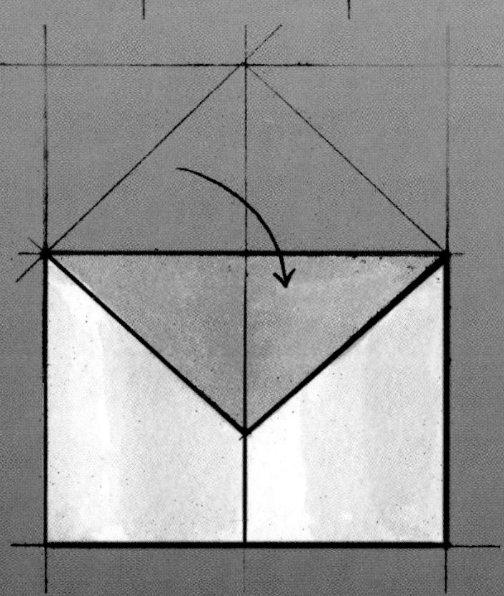

4

Take the upper right corner and bend it down to the center crease about one inch above the point facing the bottom of the paper. Crease well. Do the same thing with the upper right corner.

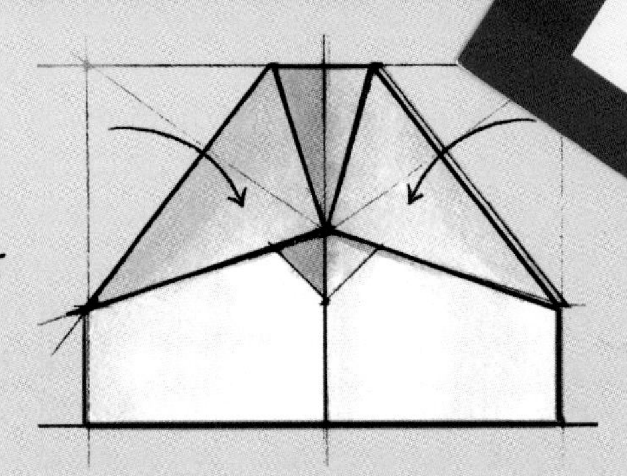

5

Take the part of the point facing the bottom of the paper and fold it up so it's right on your center crease. Flip your paper over.

6

Fold your paper in half from left to right. Be careful and make sure that the left side matches up perfectly with the right.

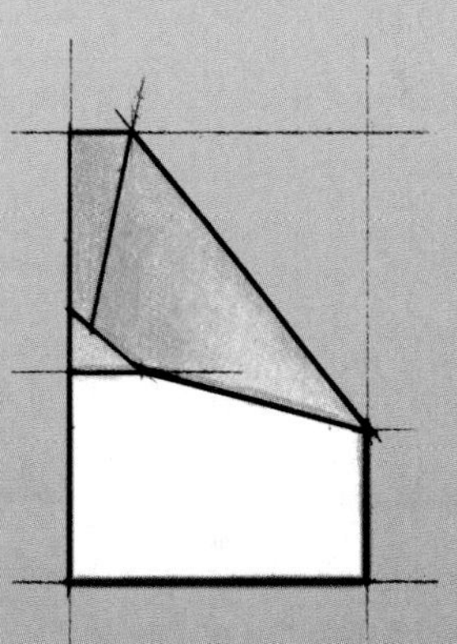

7

Make a fold so that the top flap aligns with the bottom flap. Flip over and do the same thing on the other side.

DESIGN #6

TRY THIS CONTRAPTION OUT-OF-DOORS ON A CLEAR DAY AND SEE HOW MANY KITES IT CAN CATCH.

1. Fold the piece of paper in half from top to bottom.

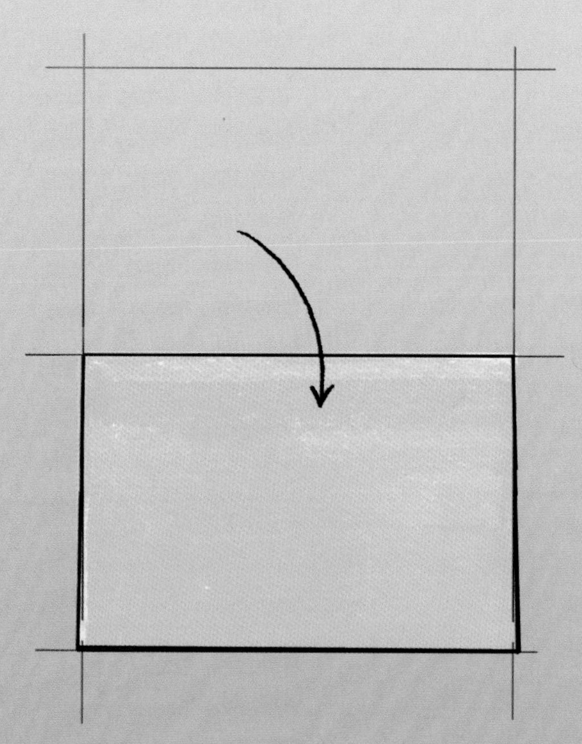

Paper airplanes hate wet weather! They will perform best in dry conditions. When the air is humid, the paper absorbs small amounts of water, causing the wings to droop and affecting the aerodynamics of the plane.

Leonardo da Vinci is cited by some (misinformed people) as the inventor of the paper airplane; in his notebooks he refers to having made a flying machine out of parchment paper.

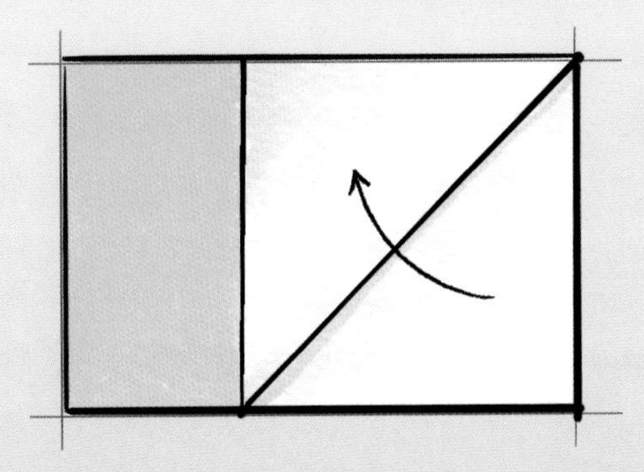

2 With the open flaps at the bottom, fold the right edge of the top flap to the crease you just made. Make it match exactly and then rub along the folded edge to make a sharp crease.

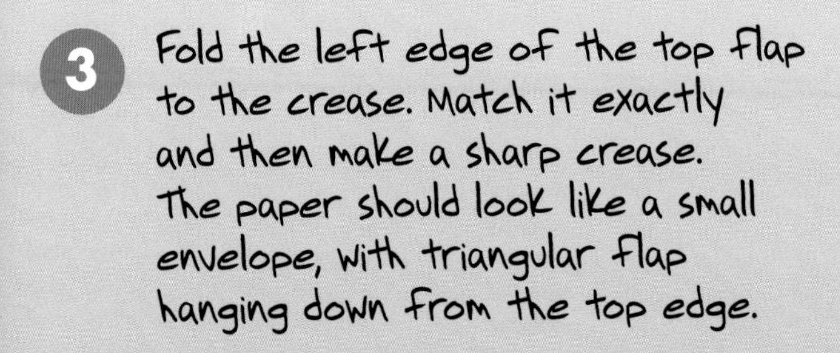

3 Fold the left edge of the top flap to the crease. Match it exactly and then make a sharp crease. The paper should look like a small envelope, with triangular flap hanging down from the top edge.

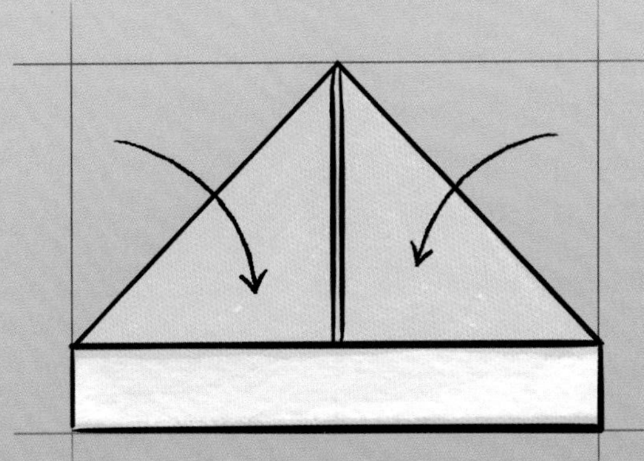

4 Fold the upper right corner down to the tip of the upside down triangle. Do the same thing with the upper left corner.

5 Unfold the last two folds. Your paper should now look like it did at the end of step 3.

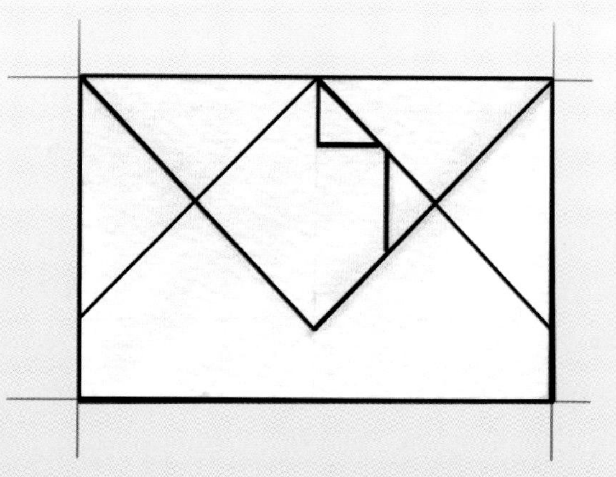

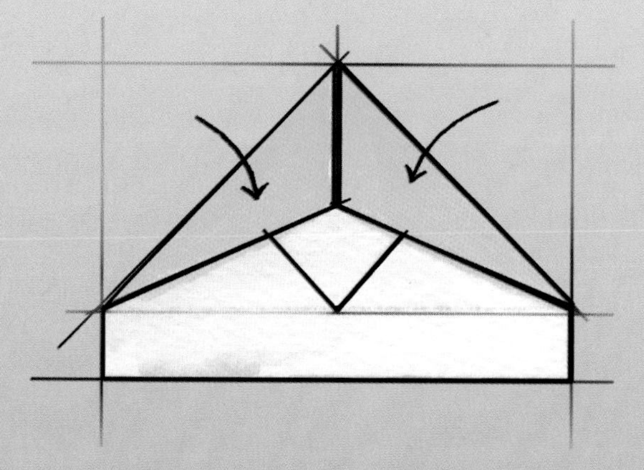

6 Fold the right and left corners down to the creases you just unfolded. The folded-down edges should almost, but not quite touch the creases. (This will make it easier to fold later.)

7 Refold along the same creases.

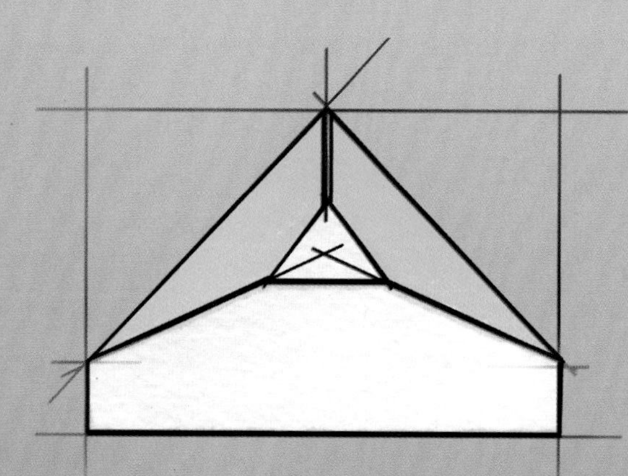

8 Fold the point that hangs down in the middle up so that the crease at its bottom is a straight line. Flip the paper over.

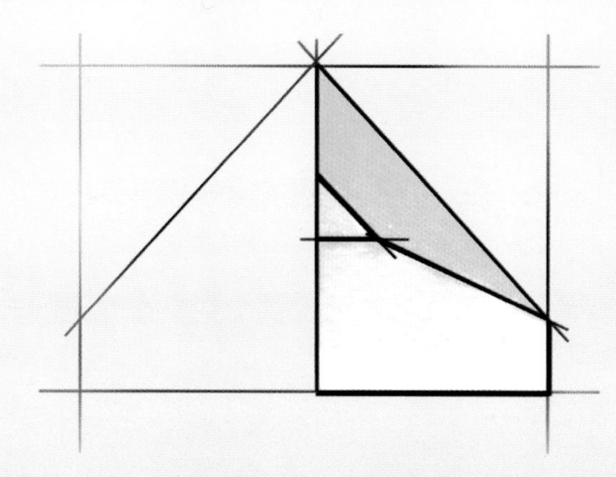

9 You are going to fold the paper in half from left to right, but before you do, carefully line up all the edges. Once it all matches up, crease your fold.

10 Fold the wings so that your plane has a sharp nose.

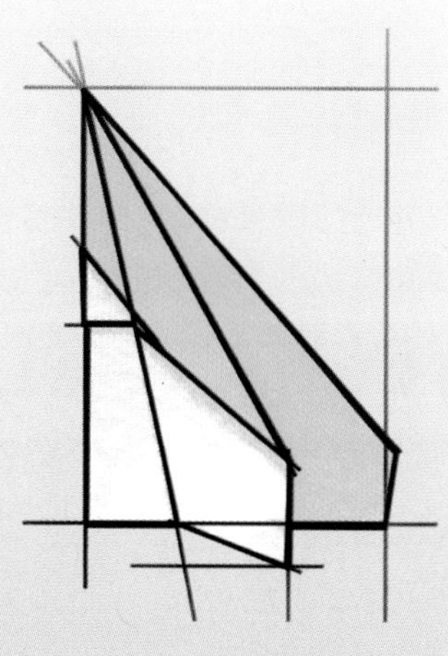

11 On each wing, make a fold about half an inch from the edge so that the edges point up.

Most paper airplane enthusiasts think that light paper airplanes will fly farther than heavy ones.

DESIGN #7

THIS FLYING MACHINE ONLY FLIES IN ONE DIRECTION — DOWN — BUT IT IS A TRUE FLYING MACHINE BECAUSE OF THE WAY IT UTILIZES AIR CURRENTS.

The WHIRLYBIRD

1

Cut a piece of paper length-wise in half so you form two skinnier, rectangular pieces of paper.

2

Take one of the rectangles and fold it in half width-wise and open it back up, so it's creased through the middle.

3

Make another crease in the paper width-wise about one inch above the center crease.

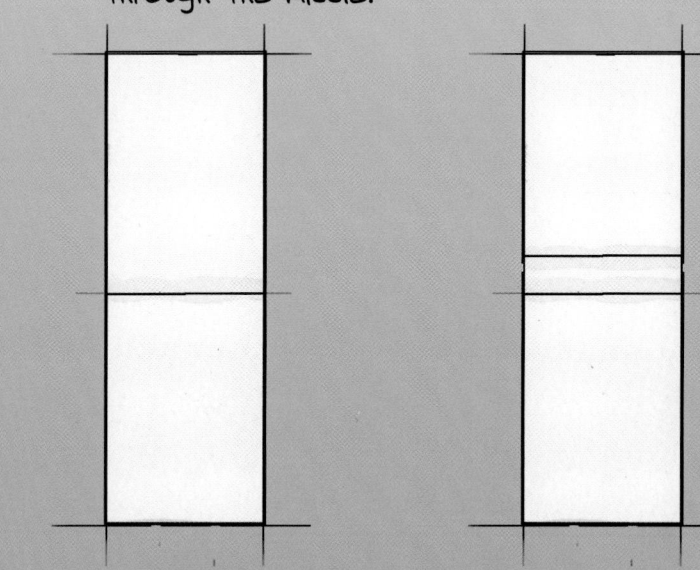

4

Using scissors, cut the paper in half above the top crease.

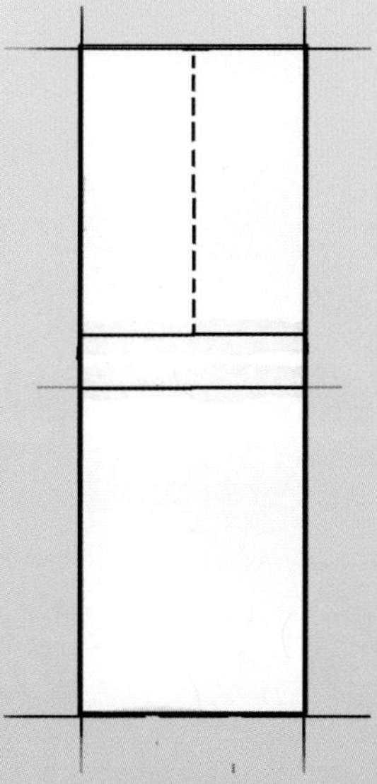

5

Then cut about 1 inch in on the right and left side of the bottom crease.

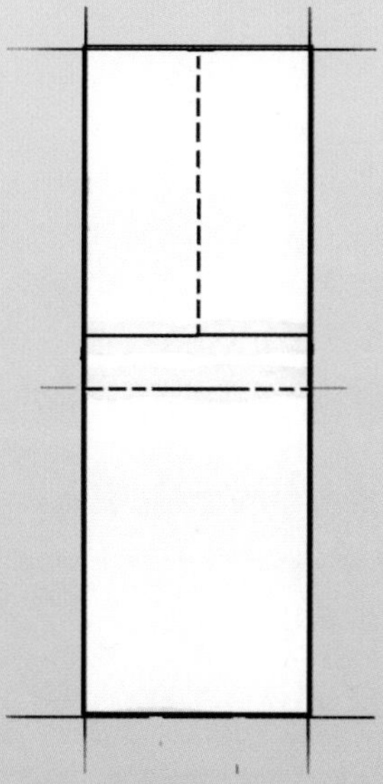

6

Fold the bottom flaps in toward each other.

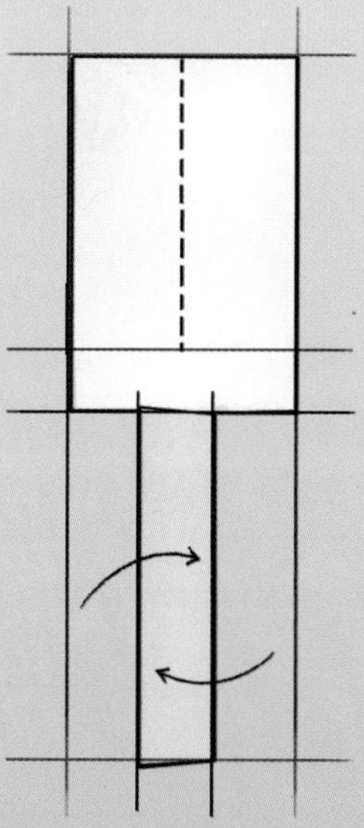

7

Fold one of the top flaps at the crease toward you and fold the other away from you.

8

Then fold the bottom flap up about 1/2 inch and fasten it with a paper clip.

For best results, hold the whirlybird by the fold of paper beneath the blades. When you let go, pull your hand out of the way very quickly!

Design #8

The Mahoney

I KEPT STARTING TO WORK ON THIS DESIGN AND THEN FOR SOME REASON I COULD NEVER FINISH IT. FINALLY I DID FINISH IT. WHEN IT WAS TIME TO NAME IT, THE NAME "MAHONEY" STUCK IN MY HEAD — ODD, BECAUSE AT THE TIME I'D NEVER MET ANYONE NAMED MAHONEY.

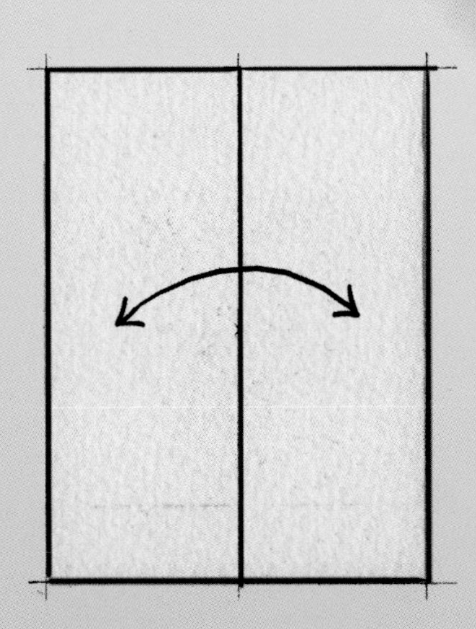

1. Take one sheet of paper and fold it in half the long way to make a crease, then unfold it.

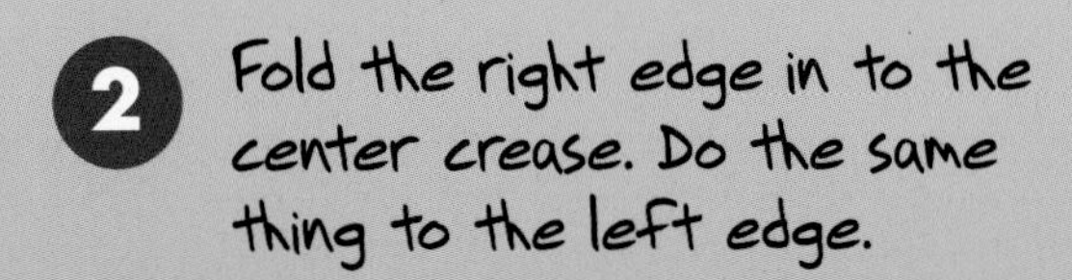

2. Fold the right edge in to the center crease. Do the same thing to the left edge.

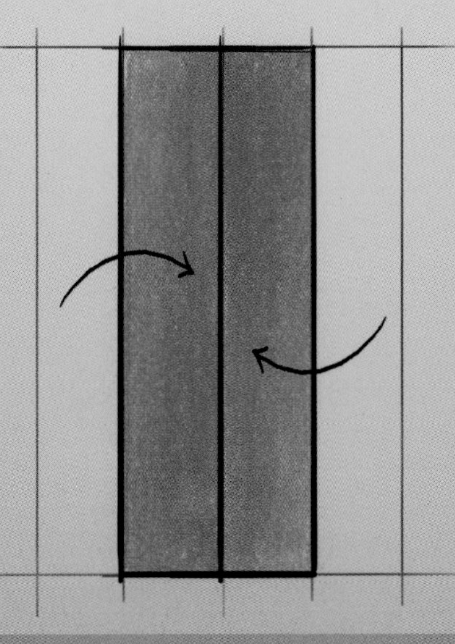

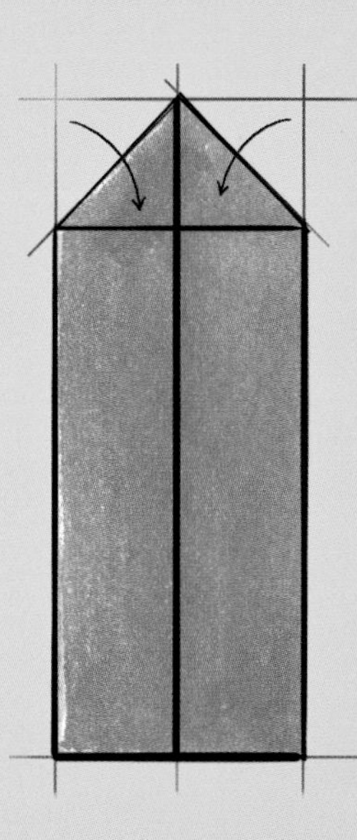

3 Fold the left top corner down so that the top edge runs along the center crease. Do the same thing to the right top corner.

4 Put your finger at the base of the triangle at the top of the paper. Then pull the big flap on the right side all the way to the right, as far as you can to make a triangle. Fold it down. Do the same thing to the other side.

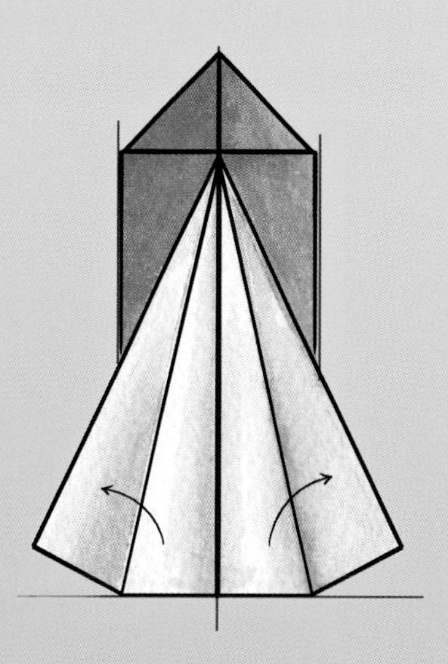

5 Flip paper over. Fold the right half over to meet the left side. The two flaps should line up.

The earliest hot-air balloons strong enough to carry human passengers were made in France in 1783 and were constructed of cloth lined with paper!

6 Open the paper up so the folds are facing you. Press it down so it lays flat.

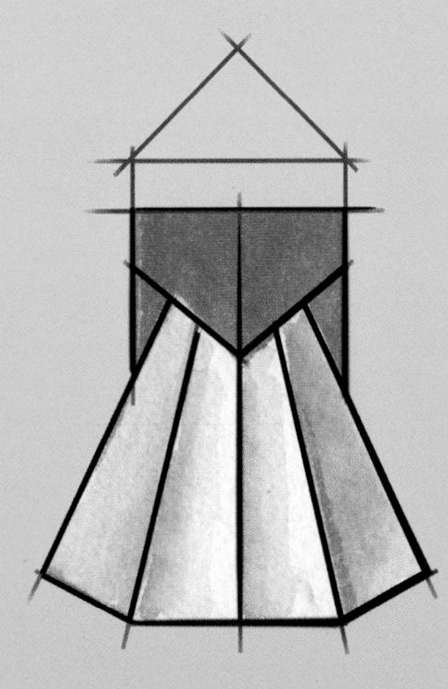

7 Fold the top triangle down and make sure the point rests on the center crease.

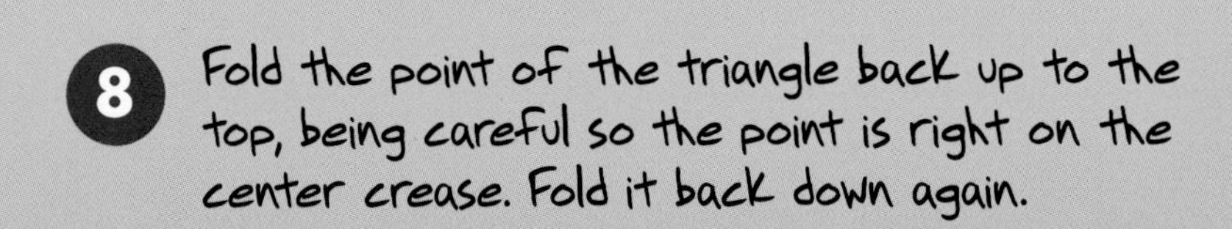

8 Fold the point of the triangle back up to the top, being careful so the point is right on the center crease. Fold it back down again.

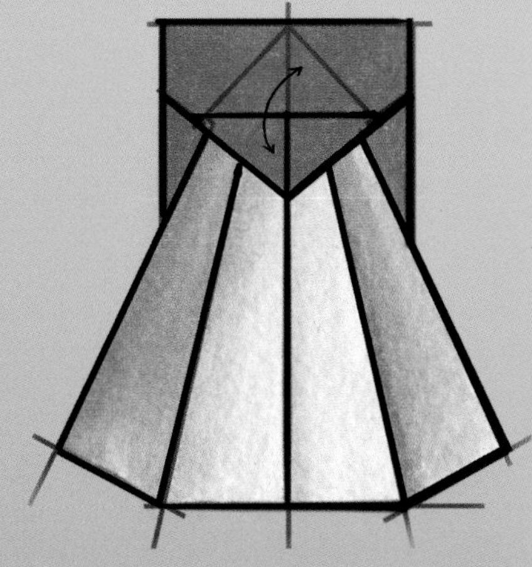

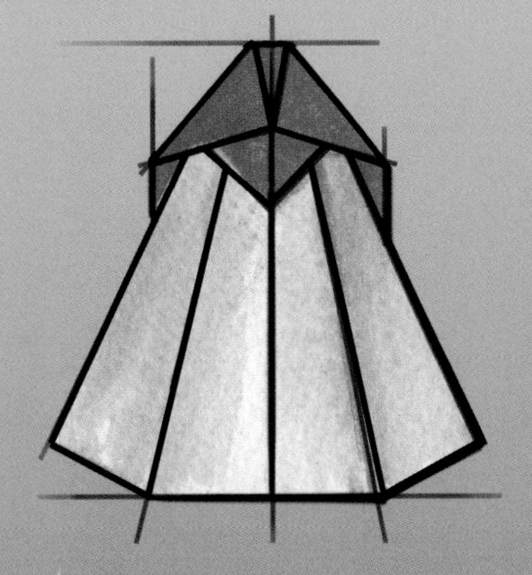

9 Take the top right corner and fold it down to the center crease. There should be a small space between the top part of your new fold and the center crease. Do the same thing with the left corner.

10 Take the point that faces towards the bottom of the paper and fold it up, make sure the tip is directly on the center crease.

11 Flip the plane over and fold it in half from left to right.

12 Fold along the red wing line. Flip it over and do the same thing on the other side. Make sure the edges on the top wing line up with the bottom wing.

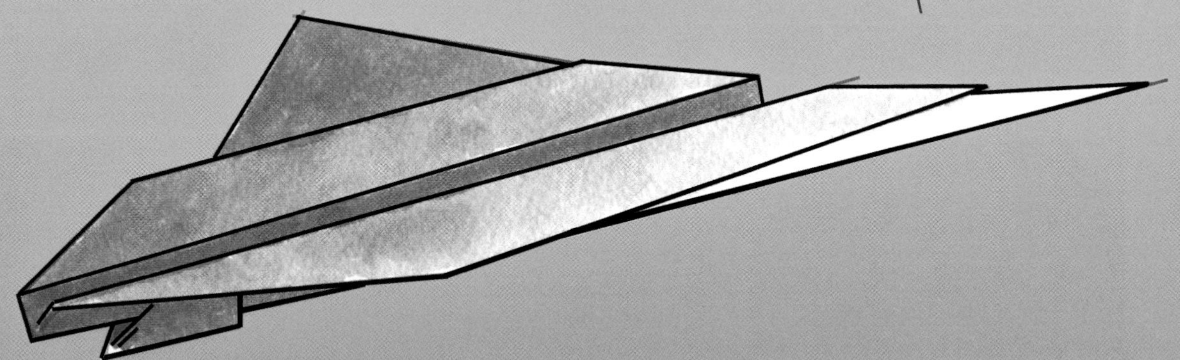

Use these pages to record the flight patterns of your contraptions. You will need a tape measure and a pencil.

NAME OF CONTRAPTION	DISTANCE TRAVELED	NOTES ON FLIGHT

Before you begin, place some kind of marker on the ground: this is where you will stand every time you throw. By always starting at the same place you will ensure accurate measurements.

NAME OF CONTRAPTION	DISTANCE TRAVELED	NOTES ON FLIGHT

Use these pages to record your own paper airplane design.

Tear out the following pages and use them to make your creased contraptions of gossamer aviation.

Here are some tips:

- Run the side of a pencil against your folds for extra sharp creases. Your planes will fly straighter.
- When throwing your planes, bend your elbow and keep your wrist as steady as possible. Your planes will stay aloft longer.
- Have fun!